# Star
## the Magic Sand Pony

*For Waldo, my North star, and for Finlay Pocket, my familiar – SK*
*To Christine – ST*

**SIMON AND SCHUSTER**
This edition published in 2015
First published in 2010 by Simon and Schuster UK Ltd
1st Floor, 222 Gray's Inn Road, London WC1X 8HB
A CBS Company
Text copyright © 2010 Sarah KilBride
Illustrations copyright © 2010 Sophie Tilley
Concept © 2009 Simon and Schuster UK
The right of Sarah KilBride and Sophie Tilley to be identified
as the author and illustrator of this work has been asserted by them
in accordance with the Copyright, Designs and Patents Act, 1988
All rights reserved, including the right of reproduction in whole or in part in any form
A CIP catalogue record for this book is available from the British Library upon request
ISBN: 978 1 4711 4422 6
Printed in China
1 3 5 7 9 10 8 6 4 2

# Princess Evie's Ponies

## Star the Magic Sand Pony

Sarah KilBride
Illustrated by Sophie Tilley

**SIMON AND SCHUSTER**

London  New York  Sydney  Toronto  New Delhi

It was a very hot day at Starlight Stables so Princess Evie
took her ponies to the shady stream to cool down.
"Who wants to come on an adventure?" she whispered as
they sipped the water. "Shall we see where the tunnel of
trees takes us today?"

You see, all of Evie's ponies were magic ponies and whenever Evie rode them, she was whisked away on a magical adventure in a faraway land.

Star looked up at Princess Evie with her beautiful blue eyes.
She was a graceful pony with a jet black coat and a
white star on her forehead.

"Yes, Star, it's your turn!" said Evie. She saddled
her pony up, grabbed her rucksack of useful things
and collected her kitten, Sparkles.

In no time at all, they were
riding towards the tunnel of trees.
Princess Evie took a deep breath.
Where would the tunnel take them today?

A warm wind blew gently through Evie's hair as they cantered out
into a huge sandy desert. A purple silk scarf fluttered around Evie's
neck and she was wearing dainty purple slippers
that curled up at the toes.

Tiny mirrors sparkled along Star's reins whilst red and gold
ribbons decorated her mane and tail.
"Look!" cried Evie, pointing. "There's a desert castle
– a kasbah! Let's take a closer look."

Princess Evie knocked on the big arched door
and a beautiful princess opened it.

"Hello! I'm Princess Zara," she smiled.
"Welcome to my home."

Zara led them to a shady courtyard and gave Evie
a refreshing cup of mint tea.

"I hope you can stay for a while," she said. "My cousins,
the seven star princesses, are coming for a sleepover and you
are invited, too. Please say you can come."

"Of course I can," said Evie, excitedly. "Sleepovers
are my most favourite things!"

As the sun began to set, Zara and Evie laid out
tasty treats for the party.
"My cousins will be here any minute," said Zara.
Evie waited patiently for a knock at the door but, instead,
there was a burst of colour in the sky above them.

A cluster of seven stars twinkled. As they grew brighter, they swirled down, leaving a glittering golden trail.

The star princesses had arrived! They were delighted
to see Zara and to meet Princess Evie. Soon, they
were all chatting and enjoying the delicious treats.

"I think it's time to get changed!" said Zara, excitedly.

The princesses rushed up to the biggest and most
beautiful bedroom Evie had ever seen. Folded neatly
on each of the beds was a pair of silk pyjamas.

"I'll lend you a pair, Evie," smiled Zara.

The princesses had a wonderful time plaiting each other's hair,
and adding beads and ribbons but, before long,
little Maya was tired. It was time for her bed.

Princess Zara tucked her up in the smallest bed
and whispered good night. Sparkles cuddled up
underneath Maya's bed and fell asleep, too.

All the other princesses tiptoed quietly back downstairs
and Zara led them to a sumptuous moonlit chamber
where little lanterns flickered. It was magical!

Some of the star princesses began to sing songs so beautiful
that soon all the others were swaying and dancing.

The princesses spun around
until everyone was quite dizzy.

They were having a fantastic time when,
suddenly, they heard a loud scream.

They raced upstairs to find Maya weeping.
"A monster with claws!" she wailed. "It was under the bed
and then it crept around the room."

Princess Zara explained that there were no such things
as monsters but then the sound of scratching claws
echoed around the room.

The princesses quickly hid behind
the curtains. A huge shadow appeared
on the bedroom wall. It had an
enormous head with enormous ears.
Its terrifying whiskers twitched.
"Aaaaargh!" cried the princesses,
as the shadow moved
towards them.

Princess Evie quickly reached into
her rucksack, pulled out a torch
and flicked on the switch.
There, in the torch's ray, was . . .

. . . Sparkles!

His huge shadow looked just like a scary monster and had
terrified Maya. "Sparkles!" said Maya, giving him a hug.
"Of course there's no such thing as monsters!"

The princesses all cuddled up in bed and
told magical stories until it was
time for Evie to go home.

She changed out of her pyjamas and said goodbye
to her new friends. But how were they going
to find the tunnel of trees in the dark?

"This magic carpet will help Star fly to the tunnel of trees,"
smiled Zara. "Don't worry, you won't lose your way!"
Zara put the carpet onto Star's back and
Princess Evie and Sparkles hopped on.

Star cantered over the sand and flew up into the sky.
Evie waved to the princesses. Then, with her torch lighting
the ground below, she spotted the tunnel of trees.

Back in the yard of Starlight Stables, Princess Evie brushed
the sand out of Star's mane, tail and coat.
"Thank you," she whispered, as Star settled down.
"That was quite an adventure!
What a magical sand pony!"

Evie skipped up to her bedroom and there, on
Evie's pillow, was a pair of purple pyjamas embroidered with
silver stars. Evie looked out of the window into the starry sky.

"Thank you!" she smiled. She was sure
the seven star princesses twinkled back!
"Miaow!" purred Sparkles, and soon
they were both fast asleep!

**Also available:**

Neptune the Magic Sea Pony
Silver the Magic Snow Pony
Willow the Magic Forest Pony
Shimmer the Magic Ice Pony
Indigo the Magic Rainbow Pony
Diamond the Magic Unicorn
Confetti the Magic Wedding Pony
Sprinkles the Magic Cupcake Pony

**Coming soon:**

Tiptoe the Magic Ballet Pony
Melody the Magic Music Pony